Taking Care of Carruthers

James Marshall

Houghton Mifflin Company   Boston

www.hmco.com/trade

Library of Congress Cataloging-in-Publication Data
Marshall, James.
Taking care of Carruthers / written and illustrated by James Marshall.
p. cm.
Summary: When Carruthers is miserable with a cold, his friends
Eugene and Emily cheer him up with a story about a wonderful adventure
they shared one summer afternoon on the river.
RNF ISBN 0-395-28593-3   PAP ISBN 0-618-07040-0
[1. Adventure stories. 2. Rivers — Fiction.] I. Title.
PZ7.M35672Tak
[Fic]
81-6619
AACR2

Printed in the United States of America
MV 10 9 8 7 6 5 4

Contents

Prologue   1

Chapter 1   The Story Begins   9

Chapter 2   Loading Up   19

Chapter 3   Shoving Off   25

Chapter 4   The Autograph Hound   29

Chapter 5   Tea and Suet   35

Chapter 6   The Mole Sisters   49

Chapter 7   The Fly and the Ointment   55

Chapter 8   A Few Old Things   67

Chapter 9   River Fever   77

Chapter 10   Wilma June   93

Chapter 11   Matinee   99

Chapter 12   Heading Home in Style   119

Epilogue   123

Prologue

At one o'clock on a wet and windy Sunday afternoon in March, three friends sat together digesting their lunch in a cozy parlor.

"What a delicious meal," said Eugene.

"Thank you," said Emily. "Baked potatoes are my specialty."

"Too bad I couldn't taste anything," said Carruthers sourly.

Eugene gave Emily a knowing look.

"Nothing worse than a cold and a sore throat," he said.

"It really spoils one's disposition," said Emily.

"There is nothing the matter with my disposition, thank you," said Carruthers.

"Of course not," said Emily and Eugene.

Carruthers sighed and gazed out at the brown and tangled garden and the grey river beyond.

"Well," said Emily brightly, "and how shall we spend the afternoon?"

"We could play Old Maid," said Eugene.

"Bo-ring," said Carruthers.

His voice was sounding scratchier.

"We could always tell jokes," said Emily. "Do you know the one about the . . ."

"Yes we do," said Carruthers. "And we don't want to hear it again."

"My, my," said Eugene.

Emily tucked an Indian blanket around Carruthers' knees.

"Mustn't get a chill," she said.

Carruthers just looked cross.

"Would you care for another throat lozenge?" said Eugene.

"They don't help one little bit," said Carruthers.

"Perhaps some tea with lots of honey?" said Emily.

"No," said Carruthers.

"Hmm," said Emily. "How unusual."

Carruthers got up from his armchair.

"I'm going for a stroll in the garden," he said.

"Oh no!" cried Eugene. "It's wet and ugly out there. You'll make yourself sicker!"

"Sit down this minute!" said Emily sternly.

Carruthers did as he was told, and Emily tucked the Indian blanket back around his knees.

Outside it was beginning to rain hard.

Eugene put another log on the fire, while Emily cleared away the dishes from the tea table.

Carruthers looked at the bewildering assortment of cold remedies and aids beside his chair. Pills, capsules, salves, syrups, vaporizer, inhaler, and tissues in three colors.

"Nothing seems to help," he said.

And then a morbid thought further darkened Carruthers' mind.

"Perhaps I'm not long for this world."

"Now, now," said Eugene.

"My stars," said Emily. "Don't be ridiculous."

"You'll be sorry when I'm gone," said Carruthers.

"Whenever I'm feeling under the weather," said Eugene, "I like to take my mind off things by reading a book."

"My eyes are too tired for reading," said Carruthers.

"I could always read out loud," said Eugene.

"Oh, I love being read to," said Emily.

Eugene went over to Carruthers' bookcase.

"There is quite a wide selection," he said. "What about this one?"

Choosing a small yellow volume, he sat down and opened to the first page.

" 'Alice was beginning to get . . .' "

"I just read that one last week," said Carruthers.

"Let's try something else," said Eugene, selecting an orange book from the third shelf.

" 'Dominic was a lively . . .' "

"Oh no," said Carruthers, "I just read that one yesterday."

Eugene tried still another.

" 'The hotelkeeper should fire that goose . . .' "

"I know that one by heart," said Carruthers.

"You must read quite a bit," said Emily.

Eugene scratched his chin.

"Well," he said, opening his briefcase, "I just happen to have brought along a story. Would you care to hear a page or two?"

"That sounds like fun," said Emily.

"It does not," said Carruthers.

"It's all about us," said Eugene.

"Hmmm," said Carruthers.

"Would you prefer it if I sang?" said Emily.

"Certainly not," said Carruthers.

"Well!" said Emily.

"You may proceed," said Carruthers to Eugene.

"This story takes place in the summertime," said Eugene.

"Good," said Carruthers. "Winter stories always put me to sleep."

"Go on," said Emily.

Eugene cleared his throat and began to read.

" 'Once upon a time . . .' "

"Humpf!" said Carruthers. "One of *those!* I like stories that really might have happened."

Eugene looked put out.

"We'll be quiet," said Emily.

And she popped a thermometer into Carruthers' mouth.

Eugene began again.

Chapter 1

The Story Begins

Once upon a time — at one o'clock on a beautiful Sunday afternoon in mid-July, to be exact — three friends — a bear, a pig, and a turtle, to be specific — sat together on the mossy banks of the Chattahoola. They were bored and had nothing to do.

"It's as dull as ditchwater around here," said the bear, whose name was Carruthers.

"You said it," said the pig, who was known as Emily.

"Nothing to do but take a nap," said the turtle, called Eugene.

Feeling drowsy in the warm afternoon sun, the three friends began to yawn and nod off.

A few feet away the milky-green river flowed lazily by, and crickets rubbed their scratchy legs together in the tall reeds.

Carruthers, Emily, and Eugene had been asleep for no more than five minutes when a loud commotion jolted them awake.

A bright red speedboat roared into view. On board was a party of frivolous fox terriers. They were laughing and carrying on and were probably drinking spirits.

"They're burying old Buzzard Watkins downriver in Skunk County!" called out the terriers. "There'll be singing and dancing all day long!"

And in a flash they were gone.

"Those fox terriers are just good-for-nothings," said Carruthers.

"There ought to be a law," said Emily.

"They seem to be having quite a bit of fun," said Eugene.

In a moment the hypnotic sound of the waves lapping the river bank had put them all back to sleep.

At first no one heard the groaning. But as the rowboat drifted nearer, the sound of terrible suffering reached their dreams, and they woke up.

"Do you see what I see?" said Carruthers.

"There is no one in it," said Emily.

"Yes there is," said Eugene, who had remarkable eyesight.

"That's just an old rag," said Carruthers.

But Eugene was not mistaken. The long white neck of a swan was draped over the prow of the boat.

Grabbing a fishing pole, Eugene pulled the boat to the bank.

"Bless your heart," said the swan, who looked decidedly ill.

As Carruthers lifted the swan out of the boat, Emily poured a glass of iced tea.

"Where am I?" said the swan after taking a big gulp.

"You are in the town of Turnipville," said Carruthers, who then introduced himself and his two friends.

The swan, who said her name was Alice, looked around.

"Land!" she cried. "Dry land!"

But when she caught sight of the river, she shuddered all over.

"Ooh," she said. "I hope I don't throw up."

Emily poured a second glass of tea, which was gratefully accepted.

When she was finally able to collect her thoughts, Alice explained that she was on her way to the birthday party of a friend downriver.

"I'm afraid I got awfully seasick," she said.

"Seasick on a river?" said Eugene.

"Whatever," said Alice.

"Isn't that unusual for a swan?" said Emily.

"Perhaps," said Alice. "But I happen to know quite a few birds who get airsick. They just don't admit it."

"You'll feel better in no time," said Carruthers. "And then you can be on your way."

"Oh no!" cried Alice. "I'll never make *that* mistake again. I'll go the rest of the way by train, thank you. Just point me in the direction of the nearest depot."

Emily offered to take Alice to the train on her motorcycle.

"That would be very kind," said Alice.

"But what about your boat?" said Eugene.

"It's yours!" said Alice. "I never want to see it again!"

"Oh, but we *couldn't!*" said Emily.

"I refuse to discuss it," said Alice. "Could I have that ride now?"

"Are you sure you are strong enough?" asked Eugene.

"I'll be all right," said Alice, averting her eyes from the river.

As Carruthers helped her into the sidecar of the motorcycle, Alice thanked everyone for her rescue.

Then Emily started up her powerful machine.

"I've never been on a motorcycle before," said Alice.

"Drive carefully," said Eugene.

In a trice Emily and Alice were in Turnipville, tearing down Main Street, heading for the depot.

"Slow down!" cried Alice.

"This is nothing," said Emily.

"There ought to be a law," muttered Alice to herself.

When Emily returned from the depot, the three friends inspected their new boat and found it sturdy.

"I have an idea," said Carruthers.

"So do I," said Emily.

"I don't see why not," said Eugene.

So they decided then and there to take a boat trip down the Chattahoola — just for the fun of it.

"It will do us good to get away," said Carruthers.

"Break up the old routine," said Emily.

"We'll have quite a bit of fun of our own," said Eugene.

Chapter 2

Loading Up

"Then let's get going!" said Emily.

"Not so fast," said Eugene. "These things take careful planning."

"Can't we just get in the boat and go?" said Emily.

"What about provisions?" said Eugene. "And maps, and life jackets? What about a camera?"

"And don't forget a first-aid kit," said Carruthers.

"Oh," said Emily.

"Now let's get organized," said Eugene.

When everyone was delegated a job, the friends agreed to meet back at the boat at one-thirty on the dot. But Carruthers and Eugene arrived to find no sign of Emily.

"I wonder what's keeping her?" said Eugene.

In a few minutes, Emily's cycle was heard coming down the road.

"She really flies," said Eugene.

"Yoo hoo!" Emily called out. "I'll need some help with this."

"That's the largest picnic hamper I've ever seen," said Carruthers.

"We don't want to go hungry," said Emily. "You know how an outing can be spoiled if there's not plenty of good food."

And she opened the hamper and itemized the contents. "One dozen deviled-egg sandwiches, one dozen fish sticks, two and a half dozen tamales, three large bags of potato chips, one large container of potato salad, a dozen chili dogs, one large container of sauerkraut, one large bottle of French mustard, and a bottle of ketchup."

"Is that *all?*" said Carruthers.

"One large Thermos of punch," continued Emily, "a pineapple upside-down cake, a dozen honey cakes, three raspberry tarts, a pecan pie, a dozen glazed doughnuts, and two dozen chocolate eclairs."

"I hope we don't go hungry," said Carruthers.

"I didn't have a lot of time!" said Emily indignantly.

"You know," said Eugene, "all this food will be too heavy for our little boat. We'll go straight to the bottom of the river."

"I never thought of that," said Emily. "Perhaps we should eat part of the contents now. That way the hamper won't be so heavy."

Carruthers explained to Emily how this

would not substantially improve the situation.

"I'm sorry," he said, "but we'll have to leave some of these provisions behind."

"I understand," said Emily, heaving a big sigh. "But don't blame me if we all faint from hunger."

"But what will we do with all the food we don't take?" said Eugene. "We can't let it go to waste. That would be wrong."

As fate would have it, a pitiful tramp happened by at that very moment.

"Can you spare something to eat? I'm down on my luck," he said, extending a mangy paw.

"We certainly can," said Eugene.

And he gave the tramp more than three quarters of Emily's provisions.

"Holy Moses!" said the tramp.

Chapter 3

Shoving Off

"Let's shove off," said Eugene.

"I'm so excited," said Emily, stepping into the boat and sitting down on the hamper.

"I shall be the captain," said Carruthers matter-of-factly.

"Very well," said Eugene. "That's fine with me."

"I beg your pardon," said Emily. "But why should *you* be the captain? Why can't I be the captain?"

"I am the captain," said Carruthers, "because I am the biggest. Now let's shove off."

But as Carruthers stepped into the boat, Emily stepped back out.

"Now see here, Carruthers," she said. "That's the worst reason I ever heard."

"I refuse to discuss it," said Carruthers. "Now get in the boat."

"Not until I can be captain," said Emily, sitting down on a rock.

"I'm sure there is a friendly way to settle this," said Eugene.

"Hush up!" said Emily.

"Keep out of this!" said Carruthers.

"Carruthers is just being juvenile," said Emily.

"*You* are spoiling our outing," said Carruthers.

"You will just have to go without me," said Emily.

"Fine with me," said Carruthers.

"Now, now," said Eugene patiently. "Everybody knows that in a rowboat whoever does all the rowing is the captain."

"Oh yes?" said Emily.

"Is that right?" said Carruthers.

"In that case," said Carruthers, "Emily can be the captain."

"I have to look after all the provisions," said Emily.

"And I have to read the maps," said Carruthers.

Eugene took up the oars.

"Then I will be captain," he said. "But only until I get tired."

The others agreed that that was fair and that it had been a silly misunderstanding over nothing.

Emily got back into the boat and opened her parasol.

"I burn easily," she said.

"Let's shove off," said Eugene.

And they did.

Chapter 4

The Autograph Hound

Rounding the first bend in the river, they immediately noticed someone at the end of a rickety pier. As they rowed closer, they made out a young hound. He was sporting a beret and dark glasses, and he was jumping up and down trying to attract their attention.

"I wonder what he wants," said Emily.

"There is only one way to find out," said Carruthers.

Eugene guided the boat alongside the pier.

The hound appeared to be more agitated

than most hounds. In addition to jumping up and down, he was biting his nails. The boaters noticed also that he was carrying a small spiral notebook and a ball-point pen.

"Ahoy," said Eugene, who wasn't sure if that was correct river talk or not.

But the hound was too excited even to say hello.

"Ooh, ooh," he said, "I can hardly stand it. Tell me quickly — are you somebody or are you not?"

"Of course we are somebody," said Carruthers. "My name is Carruthers, and these are my companions, Emily and Eugene."

"Who?" said the hound.

Carruthers repeated the names.

"Never heard of you," said the hound. "Perhaps I made a mistake. You certainly *look* like somebody. At least from a distance."

"But we *are* somebody," said Eugene.

"No, no," said the hound, becoming even more disturbed. "What I mean is, are you *some*body? Yes or no?"

"Whatever do you mean?" said Carruthers.

"Are you somebody *famous?*" said the hound in great exasperation. "Because if you *are* — famous, that is — then you shall have the honor of signing my autograph book. But of course if you are *not* famous, well then, that is an entirely different matter. So what's it going to be?"

"I'm sorry," said Eugene. "But none of us is famous."

"Not even *one* of you?" said the hound, who appeared on the verge of tears.

"Nope," said Emily.

"I should have known," said the hound. "This has been a colossal waste of my time."

"We couldn't help it," said Eugene.

"Oh, that's all right," said the hound, who had now lost all of his enthusiasm. "Most of the folks I meet are not famous. As a matter of fact, my autograph book is practically empty."

"That's too bad," said Carruthers. "But you must persevere. I'm sure someone will come along."

"That's right," said the hound, cheering up. "Better luck next time, I always say."

And he disappeared into the foliage.

Eugene rowed the boat away.

"Would you like to be famous?" he asked Emily.

"I never really thought about it," she replied. "It seems to me there are more important things."

Carruthers, however, had a faraway look in his eyes.

"Famous," he said. "Yes, it might be amusing to be famous. For a while, anyway. Until I got tired of it."

Chapter 5

Tea and Suet

Half a mile downriver Emily called everyone's attention to a stately manor.

"That must be Suet Hall," said Carruthers,
consulting his map.

"What is Suet Hall?" asked Emily.

"Surely," said Carruthers, *"you* have
heard of Ambrosia Suet, the world-
renowned writer of cookbooks."

Emily couldn't believe her ears. "Ambrosia Suet lives *there?* Ambrosia Suet, my
very favorite writer in the whole wide
world!"

"I knew you'd be interested," said Carruthers.

"Perhaps we should pay a social call," said Eugene.

"Yes, why don't we?" said Carruthers. "I've read that she is very charming."

Emily could not speak.

"On second thought, won't it be impolite, dropping in uninvited?" said Eugene.

"That's true," said Carruthers. "But perhaps if we brought her a little present, she wouldn't mind."

Emily dove into the picnic hamper. "We'll take the pineapple upside-down cake. I made it from Ambrosia Suet's very own recipe."

"I'm sure she'll be very flattered," said Carruthers.

Eugene tied the boat to a small dock belonging to Suet Hall. And Carruthers assisted Emily with the pineapple upside-down cake.

"I'm so nervous," said Emily, as they approached the house. "What will we talk about?"

"I'm sure we'll think of something," said Carruthers.

He rang the bell. But no one came.

He rang again, and again no one came.

"Maybe Miss Suet is out," said Emily.

"Miss Suet is not out; Miss Suet is in," said a sharp, thin voice overhead.

Carruthers, Emily, and Eugene looked up to see a lady peering down at them from an upstairs window.

"Miss Suet is in, but Miss Suet is not receiving guests," said the lady. "She is resting."

Carruthers did not like the lady's tone.

"Will you inform Miss Suet that three travelers have brought her a pineapple upside-down cake as a token of our esteem?"

"I'm sorry," said the lady, "but Miss Suet . . ."

"Just a minute," called out a richer, deeper voice. "Show our guests in, Miss Prune. I'll be down in a moment."

Miss Prune disappeared from the window and arrived at the front door.

"Please come in," she said in a cheerless voice. "Ambrosia Suet will be down shortly."

"Thank you," said Carruthers.

Miss Prune escorted the guests into a small sitting room.

"I'll go make lemonade," she said, leaving Emily, Eugene, and Carruthers by themselves.

"What an attractively furnished room," observed Emily, examining a large number

of watercolors of fruits and vegetables hang-
ing on the walls.

Heavy feet descended the stairs.

"Miss Suet is rather thickset, I believe,"
whispered Carruthers.

"The whole house is shaking," said
Eugene.

Emily's heart was racing. Her eyes were
glued to the door, where very shortly the

very stout Miss Suet appeared. She was
most imposing.

"Ambrosia Suet," she said in her deep
voice. "How nice of you to drop by."

Carruthers shook hands with Miss Suet
and introduced Emily and Eugene.

"How do you do?" said Eugene.

Emily found herself tongue-tied but was
able to present the pineapple upside-down
cake to Miss Suet.

"Aren't you sweet," said Miss Suet, motioning for everyone to sit down. "Isn't this a perfectly *delicious* day? Calls for some refreshments, I'd say. My assistant, Miss Olive Prune, will be along any minute with some lemonade and butter cookies to go along with this scrumptious-looking cake. You'll like Miss Prune. She helps me with all my cookbooks. We try out every recipe at least a dozen times, usually more."

Then Miss Suet took notice of Emily's skirt.

"What a lovely pistachio color you have on, my dear."

"Thank you," said Emily.

"I tend to favor citrus colors myself," said Ambrosia Suet. "Lime greens, lemon yellows, tangerine. My assistant, Miss Prune, leans toward the plum and chocolate shades."

Just then Miss Prune, pushing before her a wicker tea cart, entered the room.

"I made some finger sandwiches as well," she said dryly.

Her disposition had not seen any improvement.

"You mustn't dally too long over tea," she

said to Miss Suet. "The chapter on carrot cakes must be completed by this evening."

But Miss Suet paid her no mind. "Do try one of Prune's tasty finger sandwiches, my dears."

"What a fine house you have," said Carruthers.

"Thank you," said Miss Suet. "I have always been fond of gingerbread."

"This house is made of gingerbread?" said Emily.

Carruthers explained that in this case

"gingerbread" referred to a particular style of house built long ago.

"Yes, this house suits me just fine," said Miss Suet. "It's as warm as toast in the wintertime, and in the summer it's as cool as a cucumber. I don't go out much in the summer, of course. I have to preserve my creamy complexion, you see."

During the course of the tea party Miss Prune stood at rigid attention behind Ambrosia Suet's overstuffed chair. From time to time she bent down and whispered something in Miss Suet's ear. She also tapped her foot.

"Simmer down, Prune," said Miss Suet. "Now you've made me lose my train of thought. Where was I? Ah yes, my creamy complexion."

Leaning toward her guests, she said in a whisper, "Miss Prune here spends quite a lot of time in the sun, gardening. Sometimes she comes in as red as a tomato. But how I ramble on. I haven't even asked you three where you are going."

Emily explained how they had come into possession of their boat, and Eugene related the story of their trip so far.

Carruthers looked at his pocket watch. "Oh my," he said, "we have taken up far too much of your valuable time. We really must be on our way."

Eugene and Emily agreed.

"I see you have a camera," said Miss Suet. "Oh, do take a picture before you go."

"I'd love to," said Carruthers.

Ambrosia Suet settled back in her chair and assumed a noble pose. Emily and Eugene stood on either side, while Miss Prune remained at her post.

"Smile, Prune!" commanded Miss Suet.

"Click" went the camera.

"And now we must really be on our way," said Carruthers.

Miss Suet and Miss Prune walked their guests to the door.

Miss Suet handed everyone postcards of Suet Hall, and she gave Emily a jar of her own currant jam.

It was all Miss Prune could do to offer a civil "good-bye."

"Perhaps we may call on you sometime in the future?" said Carruthers.

"Peachy," said Miss Suet.

When the three friends were once more on their way downriver, Eugene remarked that he liked Miss Suet.

"She is a great lady," said Carruthers.

"And what an exciting conversationalist," said Emily.

Chapter 6

The Mole Sisters

"Help! Help!" screamed two moles, standing close together on a rock in the middle of the river. "Somebody save us!"

"We're coming!" cried Eugene.

"Row faster!" said Emily. "They appear to be in great distress!"

"We're coming!" repeated Eugene.

"Help! Help!" screamed the moles.

"How can we be of assistance?" said Carruthers, when they reached the rock.

At first the moles were too distressed to speak.

"However did you get out here?" said Emily.

"It was *her* fault!" cried one mole. "She's always getting us into trouble!"

"Listen to *her!*" shouted the other. "My sister is the biggest liar in the county."

"For shame!" screamed her sister. "*You* were the one who had the idea in the first place! And *now* look at us. We'll starve to death out here!"

"But, but — " said Eugene, who couldn't get a word in edgewise.

"The nerve!" shouted the second sister. "You're just trying to get out of it!"

"Hold your tongue!" snapped the other. "Or I'll give you such a smack!"

"Now ladies," said Carruthers.

But the mole sisters paid him no attention.

"I've had just about enough out of *you!*" screamed the first sister.

"Likewise, I'm sure!" said the other.

"Now hear this!" cried Emily, who was beginning to lose patience. "Do you want to get off this rock or not? We haven't got all day, you know."

The mole sisters stopped their screaming.

"Well, of course we want to get off!" they said. "Do you think it's fun being stranded out here?"

"May we row you to shore?" said Carruthers.

"That would be most kind," said the sister nearest them.

"We'll have to make two trips," said Eugene. "There's not enough room for both of you in the boat."

"Oh no!" cried the moles. "That won't do at *all!*"

"Why not?" said Carruthers.

"It's very simple," said the first mole. "We do everything together."

"We don't like to be separated," said her sister. "Not even for a minute."

"But that's *all* it would take," said Carruthers. "First we'll take one over, and then the other."

"Nothing doing," said the mole sisters. "We'd rather stay right here."

"What shall we do now?" said Carruthers in a low voice to his friends. "We can't *leave* them here."

"Certainly not," said Emily.

"There is only one thing we can do," said Eugene.

And he rowed the boat to the bank, deposited Carruthers and Emily, and returned to the rock to pick up the moles. They appeared to be very grateful to be rescued.

"We never found out how they got to be on that rock in the first place," said Emily, when they were once again on their way.

Chapter 7

The Fly and the Ointment

"We must be crossing the Skunk County line," said Carruthers, as the rowboat passed a moss-covered marker on the bank. "It's a good thing I brought *this* along."

And he reached in his satchel and drew out a large, heavy book. It was entitled, *The History of Skunk County*, Volume XXXII.

"That should provide us with all sorts of interesting information," said Eugene, who was fond of history.

"It looks dull to me," said Emily.

"Do only skunks live in Skunk County?" asked Eugene.

"Oh no," said Carruthers. "That is just a name."

"Read something out loud," said Eugene.

"Very well," said Carruthers, opening the book at random. "I shall begin reading on page four hundred and twenty-nine. 'Since the founding of Skunk County in 1867 by the notorious Colonel Cleveland J. Skunk . . .' "

"Why was he so notorious?" asked Emily, interrupting the reading.

"I have no idea," said Carruthers. "It probably explains why in an earlier volume."

"Go on reading," said Eugene.

Carruthers started over. " 'Since the

founding of Skunk County in 1867 by the notorious Colonel Cleveland J. Skunk, the inhabitants of that region have been widely known for their crafty, sneaky, low-down, no-good ways. Very few Skunk County folks can be trusted, for they are profoundly greedy, mean, and hateful; and they have a remarkable ability to tell wicked fibs and tall tales.' "

"Goodness," said Emily. "What an interesting book. Do you suppose it's all true?"

"We may soon find out," said Eugene.

Carruthers continued reading out loud. " 'The county seat of Skunk County is the dismal town of East Smudge. It is not recommended to tourists and is generally known to be a terrible place.' "

"My stars," said Eugene.

" 'Many well-known desperadoes,' " read Carruthers, " 'have come from Skunk County.' And there is a long list of names."

"Read it," said Emily, who was on the edge of her seat.

Carruthers read the list, and it was very impressive. It contained the names of:

Snakeoil Jones
Benny the Tooth
Apples "Rotten to the Core" O'Toole
Birdbrain Jenkins
Jailhouse Johnson
Weasel MacDougal
Crystal Pistol
and Louise Hopkins

"I've heard of her," said Emily.

"Here is an interesting footnote," said Carruthers. "It says here that a number of

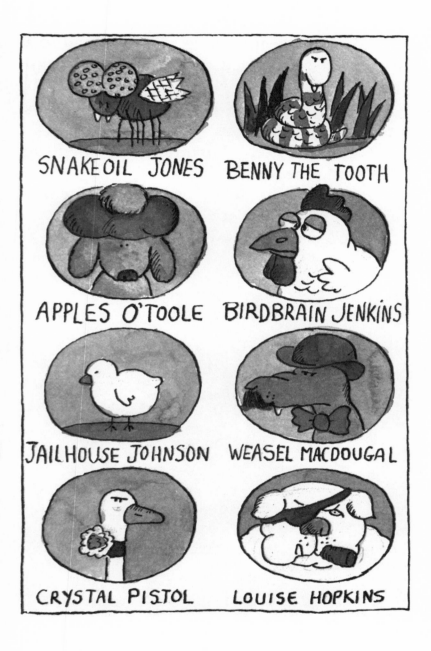

Skunk County-ites have been *so* bad that they self-combusted from general meanness."

"Ouch!" cried Emily. "Something just stung me on the nose!"

"Ouch!" cried Carruthers. "Something just stung me, too!"

"It was that horsefly," said Eugene, pointing to a buzzing black spot in the air.

"Wicked thing," said Emily.

"Here it comes again!" shouted Eugene.

The horsefly made a spectacular nose dive toward the rowboat. Carruthers ducked under an Indian blanket he'd brought along. Emily jumped inside the picnic hamper and slammed the lid shut. Eugene, who wasn't afraid of being stung, glared at the attacker.

The horsefly put on his brakes and came to a midair halt a few inches above Eugene.

"Aw nuts!" said the horsefly. "I can't sting *you!*"

"You ought to be ashamed of yourself," said Eugene. "Bothering strangers like that."

"Well, you don't expect me to sting my *friends*, do you?" replied the horsefly.

"You shouldn't sting anyone," said Eugene. "A horsefly sting really hurts."

"It certainly does!" said Emily from inside the hamper.

"I'm sorry," said the horsefly. "If you come out, I promise not to sting you."

"Promise and cross your heart," said Carruthers from under the Indian blanket.

"I promise," said the horsefly, crossing his little heart.

Emily and Carruthers came out. Both had bumps on their noses.

"Oh *my*," said the horsefly. "I'll bet that really does hurt!"

"You are awful," said Emily.

"You should be reported to the authorities," said Carruthers.

"Now, now," said the horsefly. "It just so happens that I have a remedy for that sting."

And reaching into his vest pocket, he pulled out a tiny blue bottle.

"This is my own grannie's special ointment," he said. "It's made specifically for horsefly stings. And it will cost you only one dollar."

"Never!" shouted Carruthers.

"First you sting us, and then you try to

peddle sting ointment!" cried Emily. "I've never heard of anything so nasty."

"This is how I conduct business," the horsefly said matter-of-factly.

"I'm sure it's against the law," said Eugene.

"Well, of *course* it is," said the horsefly. "I would be the shame and disgrace of the entire family if it wasn't."

"You must have quite a family," said Eugene.

"We *are* known in these parts," said the horsefly proudly. "I suppose you've heard of Snakeoil Jones?"

"As a matter of fact, we have," said Emily.

"A distant cousin on my father's side of the family," said the horsefly.

"You should be in jail," said Eugene.

"Oh, come, come," said the horsefly. "I've been in jail more times than I can count. But I always manage to get out."

"Well, you'll get no business from us," said Carruthers, reaching for his first-aid kit.

"Fifty cents!" said the horsefly. "And that's my final offer."

"No," said Carruthers, applying some ointment to Emily's swollen nose. "And *that* is final."

The horsefly put the tiny blue bottle back into his vest pocket. "Can't win them all. Well, I must be off. It's been lovely chatting with you."

"I'll just bet you're off to sting some other poor unsuspecting stranger," said Eugene.

"Natch," said the horsefly, buzzing off.

"Welcome to Skunk County," said Carruthers to his friends.

Chapter 8

A Few Old Things

It was not long before the boaters came to a reed-covered islet, in the center of which stood a tin-roofed shack. As they drew closer, they saw that the shack was inhabited. Sitting on the rundown front porch and smoking a corncob pipe was a large and ancient crocodile. He seemed unaware of them.

"Let's get out of here," said Emily.

"Now hold on," said Eugene, pointing to a wooden sign half hidden by reeds. "What does that say?"

"It probably says, 'No Trespassing,' " said Emily. "I don't like the looks of that old croc."

Eugene squinted to read the sign. "RIVER MUSEUM, ADMISSION FIVE CENTS."

"You can learn a lot in museums," said Carruthers. "I think we should look in."

"So do I," said Eugene.

"I don't think it's such a good idea," said Emily.

"Don't worry," said Carruthers. "Nothing will happen."

Eugene piloted the boat to the bank of the islet, and Carruthers helped Emily, who was already beginning to shake, out of the boat.

"Odd," said Carruthers. "The path is completely overgrown with reeds. It doesn't look as if anyone has visited in quite a while."

Who, thought Emily, would want to visit any place with a live crocodile on the porch?

It took them some time to make their way through the tall reeds. All the while, the ancient crocodile seemed not to pay them any mind.

"He's probably asleep," said Eugene.

But when they finally reached the porch, the crocodile removed his corncob pipe and tipped his straw hat.

"Afternoon," he said in a deep Southern drawl.

"Good afternoon," said Carruthers. "We have come to visit the museum."

"Sorry," said the croc. "The museum is closed on Sunday."

"Let's go," whispered Emily.

"Now, see here," said Carruthers. "Surely you could make an exception, just this once."

"Yes," said Eugene. "We love museums."

"Let's go," Emily whispered again.

"The museum is closed, and that's that," said the croc.

"Oh please," said Carruthers.

"Please," said Eugene.

Emily was dying to get away.

"Please!" she begged Carruthers.

The crocodile removed his hat and scratched his forehead. "Well," he said, "if the little lady wants to come in so badly, I suppose I could make an exception just this once."

"Wonderful," said Carruthers, handing the croc three nickels.

"Oh no," said the crocodile. "That'll cost you a quarter apiece."

"What!" cried Carruthers.

"This is a special occasion," said the croc. "Remember?"

Carruthers turned to his friends.

"We have come this far," said Eugene. "And I *do* want to see what is inside."

"Very well," said Carruthers, placing three quarters in the croc's outstretched palm.

"Thank you," said the croc. "You may go

in now and stay as long as you like. You may also take photographs."

Carruthers, Emily, and Eugene slipped past the crocodile and entered the museum. The screen door slammed behind them.

"It's very dark in here," said Eugene.

"I can't see a thing," said Carruthers.

"Let's leave," said Emily.

"Don't be so hasty," said Eugene, lighting a match.

"Don't trip over anything," said Carruthers.

"I think I see something," said Emily.

Carruthers, Emily, and Eugene were able to make out a single display case in the center of the small room.

"That looks like something important," said Eugene.

They approached the case.

"What's in it?" asked Eugene, who was hoping the case contained a shrunken head.

Everyone bent over the display case.

Three objects were on display. They were marked, "One," "Two," and "Four."

"What is that?" asked Emily, pointing to what appeared to be a small white feather.

Carruthers read the label for exhibit Number One: " 'One small white feather, probably from a goose. This feather was found floating downriver on May 1, 1883.' "

"Not very interesting," said Eugene.

"Let's look at the second exhibit," said Carruthers.

Emily read out loud, " 'One white plastic drinking cup, found floating downriver, June 10, 1957.' "

"Dull," said Carruthers and Eugene.

To the right of the second exhibit there was only an empty space. No label.

"Curious," said Carruthers.

"What's that?" said Eugene, looking at the exhibit marked "Four."

"It looks like a little pile of sand," said Emily.

Carruthers read the label. " 'One teaspoon of local silt, placed on exhibit August 3, 1903.' "

"That crocodile has his nerve," said Eugene.

The others agreed.

"I think we should leave," said Emily.

"Right," said Carruthers and Eugene, stepping outside.

"Leaving so soon?" said the old croc, chewing on the stem of his pipe.

"Correct," said Carruthers, heading for the rowboat.

Emily followed close on Carruthers' heels, but Eugene remained behind.

"Yes?" said the old croc.

"I'm curious," said Eugene, "about the third exhibit."

"Oh, that," said the croc. "I removed it

because I felt it wasn't interesting enough to put on display."

"By the way," said Eugene. "Have you lived in Skunk County long?"

"All my life," said the croc.

"I thought so," said Eugene.

Chapter 9

River Fever

"I *am* getting tired of rowing," said Eugene.

"Feeling tired and listless?" said a voice.

"Who said that?" said Carruthers, looking around.

"It is only I," said a voice.

Then the three friends noticed a raccoon paddling a small canoe toward them.

"Let me introduce myself," said the raccoon. "My name is Doctor M., and I see that you are badly in need of my services. How long have you felt devoid of energy, rundown, out-of-sorts?"

Carruthers, Emily, and Eugene looked at each other.

"We feel perfectly fine," said Emily. "Although I could do with a little snack."

"Aha!" said Doctor M. "Uncontrollable hunger. One of the first symptoms of River Fever. Aren't you lucky I happened along? Now stick out your tongues."

Opening a small black bag, Doctor M. took out a flat wooden stick.

"Say 'Ahhh,' " he said.

"We'll do no such thing," said Carruthers. "This is ridiculous."

"Hmmm," said the doctor, scratching his chin. "Irritable, aren't we?"

"Go away," said Carruthers, who had lost all patience.

"Well!" said Doctor M. indignantly. "If you don't *want* medical assistance, that's perfectly fine with me! I'm sure there are plenty of river travelers who'd appreciate a checkup by a highly competent, well-trained medical raccoon."

And without further ado, he paddled away.

"I think that raccoon *wanted* us to be sick," said Emily.

"We haven't met *one* honest creature in Skunk County," said Eugene. "That history book was not exaggerating."

"I'm honest," said a lovely soprano voice from above.

The three friends looked up and saw a pretty yellow butterfly circling the boat. "I'm as honest as can be. I *never* tell lies. Not even little white lies."

"Thank goodness for that," said Emily. "We were beginning to give up on the inhabitants of Skunk County. Everyone we have met so far has been slightly wicked."

"Isn't it awful?" said the pretty butterfly. "It just makes me sick to think of how some folks around here behave. Sometimes I say to myself, 'Rachel, folks are just too wicked around here. You'd better move away.' But then I remember how beautiful this part of the river is, and I decide to stay."

"Yes, it is very beautiful," said Emily.

"Oh, but this isn't the best part," said the butterfly. "The most beautiful part is just around the next bend. It's so calm and peaceful. You're going to love it."

"I'm sure we will," said Eugene.

"Good-bye," said the butterfly.

"Good-bye," said the three friends.

"Pleasant little creature," said Carruthers. "For a change."

Emily pulled in the oars and let the boat drift along. "I could use a quick nap after all," she said.

"Just a cat nap," said Eugene, yawning.

"Seeing so many new things can be exhausting," said Carruthers, who was also sleepy. "A quick nap will refresh us."

In no time, all three friends were snoozing away, as the boat drifted gently downstream.

Two young squirrels in a branch overhead watched them pass.

"Boy, are *they* in for a surprise," said one.

"Too late now," said the other.

And indeed it was too late, for just around the next bend lay Rip Roaring Rapids. Already the unmistakable sound of rushing water could be heard.

Emily began to mutter in her sleep.

"Somebody turn off the faucet. The bathtub will overflow."

Eugene snapped awake!

"Rapids!" he cried in fright. "Everybody hold on tight!"

In the next instant the rowboat began to pick up speed. The sound of the rushing water became deafening, and the little boat was being knocked about like a cork. First this way, then that.

Eugene turned pale with fear.

Carruthers had great difficulty keeping himself from pitching over the side. His fur was dripping wet.

The farther they went, the worse the rapids became. Next the boat began to spin round and round. Carruthers' hat flew into the air. So did Emily's parasol.

Eugene began to sweat.

Carruthers held on with all his might.

"Wheee!" cried Emily, who was enjoying herself immensely.

"Hush up!" said Carruthers. "This isn't an amusement park, you know."

"Well, it's just as much fun!" squealed Emily.

Gradually the river began to quiet down. The rapids became less and less fierce. The bumping about and spinning had stopped. Soon the deafening roar was behind them.

"We're safe now," said Eugene.

"I thought we were done for," said Carruthers.

"I could do it all over again," said Emily.

This comment drew no response from her companions.

"It was all that lying butterfly's fault," said Carruthers.

"But she looked so sweet and pretty," said Eugene.

"Things are not always as they seem," said Carruthers.

"Especially in Skunk County," said Eugene.

"Let's survey the damages," said Carruthers.

"Well, I, for one, have two scraped knees," said Eugene.

"Scraped knees? Scraped knees?" said a familiar voice. "Did I hear a call for medical assistance?"

It was the raccoon with the black medical bag.

"How did *you* get here?" asked Eugene.

"That's a medical secret," said Doctor M. "I'm not allowed to say."

When the doctor saw Eugene's knees, he seemed quite pleased. "Lovely, lovely," he said. "Now let's see, how should this be treated? Of course we could always put the knees in splints. Then again there is always traction. But perhaps I should simply operate."

"Operate!" gasped Eugene.

"What about a bandage on each knee?" suggested Emily.

The good doctor's eyes narrowed.

"You didn't tell me you had been to medical school," he said sarcastically.

"Sorry," said Emily.

"Naturally," continued the doctor, "I'll have to use some very strong anesthesia."

"But it doesn't even hurt," said Eugene.

"Cold compresses to reduce the swelling!" announced the doctor.

"But there *is* no swelling," said Emily.

"Oh, very well," grumbled the doctor. "I suppose a small bandage on each knee will do. But don't blame me if your knees fall off."

Doctor M. applied the bandages.

"And now," he said, "who else needs treatment?"

"We're fine," said Emily.

"Couldn't be better," said Carruthers.

The doctor reached into his little black bag and took out several bottles of pills and capsules.

"Just to be sure," he said, "take three of these yellow capsules four times a day for

seven days. Along with the capsules, every
hour on the hour take one of these large
purple pills for no more than sixteen days. If
palpitations *should* occur, decrease the dos-
age to one pill every six hours for thirty-
seven days. That will be a thousand dollars,
please."

Carruthers was outraged, and he said
some very strong things.

"Thieves! Thieves!" cried the raccoon. "You have taken my expert medical advice, and now you won't pay for it!"

"Here," said Carruthers, handing him a nickel. "And that's probably four cents too much!"

"Humpf!" said the raccoon. "I'll never treat *you* again!"

A quarter of a mile downstream, Carruthers pointed to another moss-covered marker.

"Look," said Eugene. "There's a sign next to it."

YOU ARE NOW LEAVING FRIENDLY
SKUNK COUNTY

"Gosh," said Eugene. "Am I ever glad to get out of there."

Chapter 10

Wilma June

"Riding those rapids really made me hungry," said Eugene.

"Me too," said Carruthers.

"Well," said Emily, looking into the hamper, "I suppose there is enough to go around."

"Why don't we stop for a picnic?" said Eugene.

His friends thought that a fine idea.

"I see a meadow up ahead," said Carruthers. "Let's stop there."

Eugene tied the boat to a tree and carried the Indian blanket to the middle of the field. Carruthers brought the picnic hamper.

"It seems lighter somehow," he said.

"A girl has to eat," said Emily.

"Are there any tamales left?" said Eugene.

"A few," said Emily.

But the tamales were all soggy.

"There's nothing worse than soggy tamales," said Carruthers.

"I wish you hadn't given that tramp all the sauerkraut and potato salad," said Emily.

Suddenly Eugene cocked his head.

"What is that sound?" he said.

"I don't hear anything," said Carruthers.

"I do," said Emily. "Someone is singing."

The three friends looked around, but they saw no one.

"That seems strange," said Carruthers.

Now the singing seemed to be coming closer.

They could make out the words of a ballad. It was all about love and flowers and the moon.

"How *very* strange," said Carruthers. "A song without a singer."

Suddenly a shadow crossed over the Indian blanket.

"I'm up here," someone said.

Carruthers, Emily, and Eugene looked up to see a hot-air balloon hovering over them. Leaning over the edge of the basket and strumming a guitar, a pretty bandicoot was looking down at them.

"Good day," said Carruthers. "And who are you?"

"Hi," said the bandicoot. "My name is Ariel Sunshine."

"What a beautiful name," said Eugene.

"Thank you," said Ariel Sunshine. "I made it up all by myself. My name used to be Wilma June, but I didn't care for it. I much prefer my new name. It suits me, and it tells everyone who I am."

"It is very original," said Eugene.

"Yes, indeed," said Carruthers.

Emily said nothing.

"And what an enchanting song you were singing," said Eugene.

"Oh, I made that up, too," said Ariel Sunshine. "I write all my songs."

"You have talent," said Eugene.

"Yes, indeed," said Carruthers.

Emily remained silent.

"I will now compose a song for my three new friends," said Ariel Sunshine. "It will be about summer and good feelings."

Ariel struck a chord on her guitar and sang a song about summer and good feelings and new friends.

"That was more beautiful than the first," said Eugene.

"Won't you land your balloon and join us

for some punch?" said Carruthers.

"Or a pickle?" said Emily.

"Oh no," said Ariel Sunshine. "I only eat nuts. But thank you anyway."

"Where are you off to?" asked Eugene.

"Wherever the wind carries me," said Ariel. "Bye-bye."

The three friends watched the balloon drift away, as Ariel Sunshine composed a song about the wind.

"Doesn't she have a thrilling voice?" said Eugene.

"Very lovely," said Carruthers.

Chapter 11

Matinee

"I see a steeple up ahead," said Emily.

It was Carruthers' turn at rowing.

"Look on the map," he said to Eugene.

"That must be Stupendousburg," said Eugene.

"Is it a big place?" asked Emily.

"I've read that Stupendousburg has a library, a bandstand in the park, and even a theater for plays," said Carruthers.

In a moment, more of Stupendousburg came into view.

"Let's stop and have a look around," said Emily.

"I'll bet there are some swell postcards in Stupendousburg," said Eugene.

Curiously, there was no one about on the Stupendousburg wharf.

"There doesn't seem to be much going on," said Emily.

"Most peculiar," said Carruthers.

"Where *is* everybody?" said Eugene.

They wandered up one street and down another. But Stupendousburg was silent and empty.

"This gives me the creeps," said Emily.

"Maybe it's a ghost town," said Eugene, who was hoping it really *was* a ghost town.

In the town square they admired the interesting old bandstand and smelled the honeysuckle bushes. Still they saw not a single soul.

"Let's leave," said Emily.

Her friends agreed, but just as they were turning to go, they saw someone hurrying toward them. It was a small red fox.

"Eureka!" cried the fox.

He was wearing a top hat, carrying a walking stick, and sporting a fresh gardenia in his lapel.

"You!" he cried, pointing at Carruthers. "Come quickly!"

"What's the matter?" asked Carruthers.

The fox dabbed at his forehead with a hankie. It was clear that he was most upset.

"I'll explain on the way," he said. "Please come! It means *everything* to me!"

"Very well," said Carruthers, "if it's all that important. But my friends must come too."

"Yes, yes," said the fox. "Now let's get a move on!"

Carruthers, Emily, and Eugene followed the fox up Main Street.

"Faster!" cried the fox. "The theater is four blocks away, and the audience is getting restless!"

"What theater and what audience?" asked Carruthers.

"The audience in the theater!" said the fox. "The audience in *my* theater! Everyone in town is there!"

"Everyone in town?" said Eugene.

"Yes," said the fox, quickening his pace. "The mayor, the judge, the sheriff! They're *all* there!"

The foursome was now hurrying along at a rapid clip.

"But what has all this to do with me?" asked Carruthers.

"It's all very simple," said the fox. "We're presenting 'Goldilocks and the Three Bears' at the theater, and one of the bears got sick at the last minute."

"Surely," said Carruthers, "you don't expect me . . ."

The fox stopped short and fell to his knees.

"I beg of you!" he cried. "Whoever heard of Goldilocks and the *Two* Bears?"

"That's true," said Emily.

Tears came to the fox's eyes. "If my play is not a success, I'll have to leave town. 'Coldilocks' is a special favorite around these parts."

"But I don't know how to act," said Carruthers.

"Nonsense," said the fox. "There is nothing to it. It's an easy part. All you have to say is, 'Who has been sitting in my chair? Who has been eating my porridge?' and 'Who has been sleeping in my bed?' "

"But I'll get nervous," said Carruthers.

"All *good* actors get nervous," said the fox.

"Well," said Carruthers, scratching his chin.

The poor fox looked very pitiful on his knees.

"I suppose I could give it a try," said Carruthers. "It certainly would be a challenge."

"It sounds like a lot of fun," said Eugene.

"I'm sure you can do it," said Emily.

"I'll do it," said Carruthers.

"I'm saved!" cried the fox.

Arriving at the theater, they heard angry voices.

"Oh dear," said the fox. "The audience is already expressing its displeasure."

Quickly they went around to the stage door and entered the theater.

Emily and Eugene stood quietly to one side as the fox introduced Carruthers to the company backstage.

"We're saved!" shouted everyone.

"I'll make an announcement to the audience that the play will shortly commence," said the fox to Carruthers. "You get into your costume."

Carruthers was shown to a dressing room.
"I'm so nervous," he muttered.

Emily and Eugene sat on a large trunk and
observed the backstage excitement.

A duck wearing a wig of bright yellow
curls rushed by.

"That must be Goldilocks," said Emily.

"I wonder which of the three bears Carruthers will play," said Eugene.

"So do I," said Emily.

A large bear wearing a straw hat and a bow tie paced back and forth memorizing his lines.

"*Who* has been sleeping in my bed?" he said in a deep, imposing voice. "Who *has* been sleeping in my bed? Who has been *sleeping* in my bed?"

"That must be Papa Bear," said Eugene.

"Where is my throat spray?" cried a large lady bear. "And why aren't there any flowers in my dressing room?"

"Mama Bear," whispered Emily to Eugene.

"Uh oh," said Eugene. "You know what *that* means."

The door to Carruthers' dressing room opened slowly.

"Here he comes," said Emily.

"Whatever you do," said Eugene. "Don't giggle."

"Of course not," said Emily.

Carruthers emerged from his dressing room wearing his Baby Bear costume.

"I feel foolish," he said.

"You look fine," said Eugene.

"Curtain going up in two minutes!" cried the fox.

"I think I'm too big for this part," said Carruthers.

"Well, yes," said the fox. "But we can't do anything about that now. Just speak in a high squeaky voice, and maybe the audience won't notice. A good actor can make an audience believe *anything*."

"I'll do my best," said Carruthers.

"That's the spirit," said Eugene.

"Break a leg!" shouted the duck who was playing Goldilocks.

"What an awful thing to say!" exclaimed Emily.

Eugene explained that "Break a Leg" is an expression used by actors to mean "Good Luck."

"Oh," said Emily.

"Curtain going up!" shouted the fox.

Emily and Eugene held their breath.

With a soft whirring noise the curtain rose, and the audience applauded the set, which represented the inside of the house of the three bears.

"You're on," whispered the fox to Goldilocks. "Break a leg!"

The duck skipped on stage and was immediately met with applause.

"She is the star of the show," whispered the fox to Emily and Eugene.

Emily and Eugene watched the duck's acting with interest.

"She really isn't very good," whispered Emily to Eugene.

"I think she is making up some of her lines," whispered Eugene.

On stage the duck was getting confused.

"Why, Grandmother," she said to a bowl of porridge, "what big eyes you have!"

Suddenly there was quite a lot of hissing in the audience.

"Oh dear, oh dear," said the fox, who was in a terrible state. "She has forgotten what play she is in!"

But in a moment the duck remembered

her correct lines, and the audience settled down.

When it came time for the three bears to appear, both Emily and Eugene moved to the edge of the trunk.

"This is it," whispered Eugene.

"Break a leg," whispered Emily.

At this point the fox had fainted dead away and had to be revived with a pitcher of water.

But Papa Bear, Mama Bear, and Baby Bear performed beautifully. They forgot none of their lines, and they acted up a storm.

It was a splendid performance.

"Carruthers is the best of all," whispered Emily.

"I knew he could do it," whispered Eugene.

When the final curtain came down, the audience went wild. They shouted "Bravo!" They whistled. They threw their programs in the air.

"My, my," said the fox. "What a triumph! Your friend can really act!"

"But of course," said Emily and Eugene proudly.

Each of the actors took a solo bow.

Goldilocks, in spite of all her mistakes, was roundly applauded.

Papa Bear was roundly applauded.

And so was Mama Bear.

But when Carruthers took *his* bow, the ovation was stupendous.

"Bravo! Bravo!" shouted the audience.

Someone even threw a bouquet onto the stage.

"I've never seen anything like it," said the fox.

When all the shouting had finally died

down, the mayor and the dignitaries of the town appeared backstage. Everyone crowded around Carruthers, and Emily and Eugene were as proud as could be.

"I'm so glad we decided to stop off in Stupendousburg," said Emily.

"So am I," said Eugene.

The crowd around Carruthers grew larger. Everyone wanted to have a look at the gifted actor.

"Let me through!" someone demanded.

"I know that voice," said Eugene.

It was the hound with the notebook, and he was having a hard time making his way through the throng.

"Well!" he said in an exasperated voice when he finally got to Carruthers. "You told me you were nobody! And now the whole town is talking about you!"

"It's nothing," said Carruthers. "I was just filling in."

"You *must* sign my book!" said the hound. "I'd be ever so grateful!"

"Very well," said Carruthers, accepting the hound's pen.

Now everyone was clamoring for autographs.

Carruthers politely signed programs and then quietly excused himself.

"I must be going," he said. "My friends need me."

Everyone looked at Emily and Eugene with envy.

"I feel rather important myself," whispered Eugene to Emily.

Outside the theater a large crowd of citizens was waiting. They hoisted Carruthers, Emily, and Eugene into the air and carried them to the wharf.

"Good-bye! Good-bye!" called out the crowd as the rowboat pulled away.

"Well, Carruthers," said Eugene. "What's it like to be famous?"

"It's very nice," said Carruthers, "but I wouldn't want to do it every day."

Chapter 12

Heading Home in Style

"My stars!" said Eugene. "Just look at the time!"

"The sun is setting," said Emily.

"And we are quite a long way from home," said Carruthers.

Eugene turned the boat around and headed home.

"We'll never make it back before nightfall," said Carruthers.

"And I'll bet that old crocodile up in Skunk County is just waiting for us," said Emily.

"We *could* spend the night in Stupendousburg and go home in the morning," said Eugene.

"Oh no," said Carruthers. "I don't like sleeping in strange beds."

"Neither do I," said Emily.

"Well, in that case," said Eugene, "we'll have to really step on it."

They had not gone far, however, when they encountered the speedboat full of the fox terriers, who clearly did not know when to quit.

"Old Buzzard Watkins really went out in style!" they shouted. "And the party is still going on!"

Eugene had an idea.

"We need your help!" he called to the terriers.

(For everyone knows that, although frivolous and devil-may-care, fox terriers are always willing to lend a paw.)

"Yes?" said the terriers, pulling alongside the rowboat.

"Will you tow us upriver as far as Turnipville?" asked Eugene.

"Sure," said the head terrier. "But we go like the wind."

"We'll hang on tight," said Carruthers.

Eugene tossed a rope to the terriers, and the three friends held on for dear life.

"This is going to be wild!" cried Emily, who was no stranger to speed.

With a terrific roar, the speedboat tore upriver, pulling the rowboat and its three passengers behind.

"I can't look," said Carruthers.

"This is more fun than the rapids," said Emily.

The lights of Skunk County were just twinkling on as they sped past.

Emily was sure she could make out the yellow eyes of the museum director peering at them from his front porch.

"Look!" said Carruthers. "There's Turnipville up ahead. We really made time."

"I think I prefer traveling at a slower pace," said Eugene, who was slightly dizzy.

Signaling the terriers to drop the line, they rowed to the riverbank and home.

Epilogue

Outside the wind had died down, and the rain was now only a drizzle.

"Did you like the story?" said Eugene.

"Yes indeed," said Emily. "I can hardly *wait* for summer."

"How do you feel now, Carruthers?" said Eugene.

But Carruthers could only mumble.

"Oh my," said Emily. "I forgot about the thermometer."

Emily took the thermometer out of Carruthers' mouth and read it.

"You don't have a fever," she said.

"I feel somewhat improved," said Carruthers.

"Perhaps this summer we really will take a trip downriver," said Eugene.

"Remind me to pack a big lunch," said Emily.